THE ITALIAN TWINS by Lucy Fitch Perkins.

Lucy Fitch Perkins was forty-eight when she was approached by a publisher friend who, impressed by her talents as both an illustrator and writer, which he knew through correspondence, urged her to write. He was so earnest that she thought of an idea for a children's book the next morning, and she immediately set to work making sketches and preparing the idea for presentation. The publisher came to dinner at their house the next evening and she showed him the idea. His response was immediate "go ahead and write it, and I want it". That book was The Dutch Twins, the first in what became a long running and wildly popular series. Here we publish another in that series 'The Italian Twins'.

Index Of Contents

CHAPTER I. MORNING IN THE GRIFONI PALACE.

Near the banks of the river Arno, in an upper room of the beautiful old palace of the Grifoni family, Beppina, the twelve-year-old daughter of the Marchese, lay peacefully sleeping. In his own room across the hall from hers, Beppo, her twin brother, slept also, though it was already early dawn of Easter Saturday in the city of Florence, and both children had meant to be up before the sun, that no hour of the precious holiday should be lost in sleep.

It was the jingle of donkey bells and the sound of laughing voices in the street below her windows that at last roused Beppina. Though it was not yet light, the peasants were already pouring into the city from outlying villages and farms, bringing their families in donkey-carts or wagons drawn by sleek oxen, to enjoy the wonderful events which were to take place in the city on that holy day.

Beppina opened her great dark eyes and sat up in bed to listen. "I'm awake before Beppo," she whispered joyfully to herself. "I told him I should be first. I wonder what time it is!"

As if in answer to her question a distant clock struck five. "Five o'clock!" murmured Beppina, and, struggling to her knees in her great carved bed, she dipped a dainty finger in the vase of holy water which hung on the wall near by, and crossed herself devoutly. Then, folding her hands, she murmured an Ave

Maria before the image of the Virgin which stood on the little table beside her bed. This duty done, she slid to the floor, thrust her little white feet into a pair of blue felt slippers, and her arms into the sleeves of a gay wrapper, then ran across the room to the eastern windows.

As she pushed open the shutters, a gleam of sunshine flashed across the room, lighting the dim frescoes on the high ceiling, and paling the light of the little lamp which burned before the image of the Madonna. A wandering breeze, fresh from the distant hills, blew in, making the flame dance and flicker and flaunting a corner of the white counterpane gayly in the air.

Beppina leaned her arms on the wide stone window-sill, and looked out over Florence. The sun had just risen above the blue crest of the Apennines, its level rays tipping the Campanile and the great dome of the Cathedral with light, and turning eastern window-panes into flaming beacons. The glowing colour of the sky was reflected in the waters of the Arno, which flowed beneath its many bridges like a stream of molten gold. Pigeons wheeled and circled above the roofs, and the air was filled with gentle croonings and the whir of wings.

For a moment Beppina stood drinking in the freshness of the lovely spring morning, then, stepping softly to the door of her room, she opened it cautiously and peered into the dark corridor. She listened; there was not a sound in the house except the gurgle of a distant snore.

"Ah, that Teresina!" murmured Beppina to herself. "She sleeps like a kettle boiling! First the lid rattles, then there is a whistle like the steam. Why does she not put corks in her nose at night and shut the noise up inside of her?"

She slipped silently into the hall and listened at the door of Beppo's room. She heard no sound, and was just on the point of turning the knob, when the door flew open of itself and a boy with great dark eyes like her own burst into the corridor and bumped directly into her.

Beppina backed hastily against the wall, and though the breath was nearly knocked out of her, remembered to offer him her Easter greetings.

"Buona Pasqua, Beppo mio," she gasped. "I was just going to wake you."

"To wake me!" Beppo shouted derisively. "That's a good joke. I'm up first, just as I said I should be! See, I am all dressed, and you, you have not even begun!"

Beppina laid her finger on her lips. "Hush, Beppo!" she whispered. "Don't roar so. It's only five o'clock, and every one else in the house is asleep. Not even the maids have stirred, and as for Teresina, listen to her! She sleeps like the dead, though less quietly, yet she rouses at once if the baby stirs, and if we should wake the baby at this hour, she would be angry at us all day long."

They listened for a moment to the appalling sounds which rolled forth from the room where Teresina, the nurse, slept. Then Beppo said: "If the baby can sleep through that noise, she can sleep through anything. It sounds like a thunderstorm in the mountains."

At that moment a wicked idea popped into his head. "I know what I'm going to do," he whispered, grinning with delight. "I'm going to creep into her room like a cat and drop something into her mouth. She sleeps with it open, and I have a piece of soap just the right size!"

"Beppo!" gasped Beppina. "Don't you dare! Teresina would then refuse to take us to the piazza, and you know very well there is no one else to go with us, for the governess had a headache last night and went to bed looking as yellow as saffron."

"Oh, but just think how funny Teresina would look, choking and sputtering like a volcano pouring forth fire, smoke, and lava," chuckled Beppo, who was studying geography and liked it much better than Beppina did.

"If you do it you'll just have to spend Easter Saturday in the house and miss all the fun," warned Beppina. "Mammina would not let us go with any of the other servants."

"I don't see why she won't let us go alone," said Beppo crossly. "I hate to go out on the street with Teresina all dressed up in her ruff and streamers so people will know she's a baby nurse. I'm big enough to go by myself!"

Beppina looked despairingly at her brother. "Oh, dear!" she said, "I wish Mammina had taken us with her to the villa instead of leaving us to go later with Teresina and the governess, when she has everything ready for us. I wouldn't mind missing Easter Saturday here if only we could be up at the villa."

"Or if only our dear Babbo had not had to go away to Rome," added Beppo gloomily. "He would have taken us with him to see all the Easter sights, and no thanks to Teresina either!"

"But they did go, both of them," sighed Beppina. "So it's Teresina or stay at home for us, and I'm sure I don't want to stay at home!"

Beppo thrust his hands into his pockets, hunched up his shoulders, and looked so gloomy and obstinate that Beppina saw something must be done at once. "Oh, pazienza, Beppo mio!" she said, giving him a little shake. "It might be worse surely. Come, let's go down to the garden and feed the pigeons. You get the crumbs while I dress."

"Hurry, then," said Beppo, brightening a little, as Beppina flung him a butterfly kiss and ran back to her room. She threw on her clothes in two minutes, fastened her long black hair with a hair-pin, and appeared again in the corridor just as Beppo returned from the kitchen with a pan of crumbs in his hand.

The two children then quietly opened the door which led from the Grifoni apartment into the public hall of the old palace and crept silently down the long, dark stone stairs to the ground floor, where Pietro, the porter, lived with his wife and six children. Pietro opened the door of his own apartment and stepped into the public hall just as the two dark figures came stealthily down the last flight. Beppo was certainly in a mood for mischief that morning, for when he saw Pietro he crept softly up behind him as he was buttoning the last button of his livery, and suddenly shouted "Boom!" right in his ear!

Pietro thought it was one of his own children who had played this saucy trick. "Santa Maria!" he cried, wheeling about with his hands out to catch and punish the offender. "Come here, thou thorn in the eye!" Then, as he saw the children of the Marchese grinning at him out of the shadows, his hand went up in a salute instead. "Buona Pasqua, Donna Beppina!" he cried, "and you too, Don Beppo! Why are you about at this hour in the morning scaring honest people out of their wits?"

"Buona Pasqua, Pietro," laughed the Twins. "We are going out in the garden, and we want you to open the door for us."

No one but the gardener and the members of the Grifoni family ever went into the garden, which lay at the back of the palace, for the tenants who occupied other portions of the ancient building were not allowed to use it, and the Marchese Grifoni lived in Florence only during the winter months. The rest of the year, and the children thought much the best part of it, was spent in their beautiful vine-covered villa in the hills near Padua.

Pietro selected a key from the jingling bunch which he carried at his belt, and opened the old carved door. It was a charming sight which greeted their eyes as the door swung back on its rusty hinges. The garden was small, with a high wall all about it, over which ivy spread a mantle of green. In the middle of the space a fountain splashed and bubbled, and the garden borders were gay with yellow daffodils, blue chicory, and white Florentine lilies. There were other delights also in the Grifoni garden, for in the fountain lived Garibaldi, a turtle of great age and dignity, and in the chinks of the walls were lizards which liked nothing better than to be tickled with straws as they lay basking in the sunshine.

The moment the children appeared, a cloud of pigeons swept down from the neighbouring roofs and begged for food. Beppina held a piece of bread between her lips, and a fat pigeon with glistening purple feathers on his breast instantly lit upon her shoulder. He was followed by another and another, until she flung up her arms and sent them all skyward in a whirl of wings, only to return again a moment later to peck the morsel from her lips.

As she was playing in this way with the pigeons, she chanced to glance up at the windows of the porter's rooms which overlooked the garden. There, gazing wistfully out at them, were six pairs of eyes, belonging to Pietro's six children. Beppina waved her hand at them. "Come out!" she cried gayly, and, wild with delight at such an unheard-of privilege, the six came scrambling into the garden at once. There the eight children played with the pigeons in the sunshine, until in an unlucky moment Pietro's youngest baby fell into the fountain and was rescued, screaming with fright, by Beppina, who got her own dress quite wet in the process.

It was at this very moment, as luck would have it, that Teresina appeared in the doorway, her ruffled cap bristling and her hands upheld in horror at finding the children of the Marchese Grifoni playing in the sacred palace garden with the dirty little children of the porter's family.

"I have been looking everywhere for you," she said with freezing dignity. "The priest will soon be here to bless the house, and you, Signorina, are not half dressed, and besides, you are as wet as if you had been swimming in the fountain! What would the Signora say if she could see you now?" She glared at the six children of Pietro as she spoke, and they instantly scuttled back into their own quarters like mice who had seen the cat. Then she thumped majestically upstairs.

The children prepared to follow, but all the brightness had gone out of the morning, and they went slowly and sullenly. Though Teresina had a good heart, she had a sharp tongue, and the Twins had some reason for not loving her. It was now six months since she had first appeared before them, carrying a little red, wrinkled baby on a pillow, and had told them that it was their little new sister, and that now the Signora, their mother, would love the baby much better than she loved them, and she had laughed when she said it! Yes, believe it or not, she had laughed!

"Teresina is always spoiling things," said Beppo, kicking his feet against each step as he began to climb the stairs.

"Che, che!" said Beppina, which is Italian for "tut, tut."

"After all, it is quite true that we must be ready for the priest. What would Mammina say if she knew we were wet and dirty when he came?"

Beppo's face broke suddenly into a beaming smile. "I know what I'll do!" he cried, and disappeared into the garden again. In a moment he came back, carrying some water from the fountain in an old flower-pot, and went bounding upstairs two steps at a time, slopping it all the way.

Beppina followed breathlessly, and reached the top step just in time to see that bad boy give a vigorous pull at the bell.

There was a scrambling sound within before the door was thrown open by Teresina, who, supposing it to be the priest, had instantly called the other servants and flopped down upon her knees to receive his blessing, and the sprinkling of holy water which always accompanied it. Behind Teresina knelt Maria, the cook, and Antonia, the house-maid, with their hands clasped and their heads reverently bent, and it was only when they had all received a generous dose of water which was not at all holy that they raised their heads and saw the grinning face of Beppo and the empty flower-pot in his hand. Teresina started wrathfully to her feet, and if the real priest had not been heard coming up the stairs at that moment things might have gone badly with Beppo. As it was, the real priest followed the bogus one so quickly that there was just time for the children to slip to their knees before Padre Ugo, who was short, fat, and breathless, entered, followed by an acolyte carrying the vessel of holy water.

Padre Ugo was in a tremendous hurry, for he had many other places to visit that morning. He fairly ran through the rooms, sprinkling each with a dash of holy water, mumbling a prayer and raising his hand in blessing, then racing on to the next, with all the household trailing behind him like the tail of a kite. He blessed the kitchen and pantries, he even blessed the cat which was washing her face by the kitchen range. Not being a religious cat, she put up her tail and fled into the coal-hole, where she stayed until the priest had gone.

The only room in the whole house to be missed was the one occupied by the governess. That poor lady had locked herself in with her headache, and she was a Protestant besides, so that room had to go unblessed the whole year through.

When Padre Ugo had gone, Teresina was obliged to give her whole attention to the baby, and it was not until she and the Twins were ready for the street that at last she said stiffly to Beppo, "To-morrow morning, Don Beppo, you will find that the hares have left no Easter eggs in the garden for such a naughty boy as you."

CHAPTER II. IN THE PIAZZA.

The clock in the reception hall had already struck eleven, when the two children, dressed in their best, followed by Teresina, passed out beneath the carved stone arch of the palace door into the streets of Florence. Their way lay through the edge of the beautiful Boboli Gardens, where lilacs bloomed, and birds were singing as they built their nests, past churches and palaces, across the Ponte Vecchio, one of the oldest of all the old bridges across the Arno, and then on through narrow streets on the other side of the river, and it was nearly noon when at last they reached the Piazza del Duomo.

The square was a wonderful sight on that beautiful spring morning. There in front of them rose the great Cathedral, with its mighty dome, and beside it stood the bell-tower, which Beppina had watched from her window in the dawn. Here also in the square was the old Baptistery, il bel San Giovanni, where Beppo and Beppina, and all the other children in Florence had been baptised when they were babies.

From all the side streets entering the piazza there poured streams of people, until it seemed as if everybody in the world must be there. In that great crowd there were peasants leading donkeys, with bells jingling from their scarlet trappings; there were carts filled with black-eyed babies and women whose only head-covering was their own sleek black braids; there were farmers and peddlers, noblemen and beggars, great ladies and gypsies, bare-footed monks and tourists, black-hooded Brothers of the Misericordia, and organ-grinders, fruit-sellers, flower-sellers, old people and young, rich and poor, every one eager for the great Easter spectacle to begin.

Teresina found a place for the children and herself on the edge of the crowd, and almost at once there appeared right before their eyes a great black car drawn by four splendid white oxen all garlanded with flowers.

This strange black car stopped directly in front of the Cathedral; then from the open door of the Baptistery came a solemn procession, headed by the Archbishop bearing a brazier filled with sacred fire. The procession disappeared within the Cathedral doors, and there was a moment of breathless silence both within the church and without, as the Archbishop lighted the candles on the high altar from the holy fire.

The instant the candles flamed, the choir burst forth in a great swelling chorus. "Glory to God in the highest," they sang, and the bells in the Campanile began to ring as if they had suddenly gone mad.

Then the wonderful thing happened for which every one had been waiting. Out of the door of the Cathedral, high above the heads of the people, there flashed a white dove! It sped along a wire to the great black car, and the instant it touched it there was a terrific bang, then another, and another, as hissing rockets tore their way into the sky. The whole car seemed to blow up in a joyful burst of sound!

"Look! Look! the Colombina!" shouted the people, and as the mechanical dove returned along its wire to the altar, the air was filled with shouts of "Christ is risen! Buona Pasqua! Buona Pasqua!" from a thousand throats.

The bells of the Campanile clashed and sang overhead, waking all the bells in Florence and in the hills for miles around, so that, with the singing and the ringing, there was never a more joyful noise made than was heard in the Piazza del Duomo on that Easter Saturday in Florence!

Teresina and the children, shouting like the others, had just turned with the crowd to follow the car as it moved away from the Cathedral doors, when suddenly Teresina gave a shriek of joy, and, dropping their hands, rushed to the side of a cart which was standing beside the curb in one of the streets opening into the square. It is not surprising that she forgot the children for a moment, for there in the cart sat her mother, holding in her arms Teresina's own baby, which she had left at home in order to take care of the baby of the Marchesa. Moreover, beside the cart was Teresina's husband, and in it there were also her little brothers and sisters!

The Twins, thus suddenly loosed from Teresina's grasp, were swept along by the crowd, and when, a few moments later, she turned to look for them, they were no longer in sight.

Beppina clutched Beppo's arm as they were pushed along by a fat man behind them. "We must find Teresina!" she shouted in his ear.

"We can't get back!" Beppo shouted in reply, punching the fat man in the stomach with his elbow and pulling Beppina closer to his side; "and besides," he went on in a lower key, "I'm glad to get away from her. We'll have a good time by ourselves and go home when we get ready without being followed around by a nurse like two babies."

"What will Mammina say?" gasped Beppina.

"She isn't here, so she won't say anything at all," said naughty Beppo. Then he added with an important wag of his head; "Just you stick by me; I'll take care of you."

Beppina had her doubts, but she considered Beppo the most remarkable boy in the world, so she trotted obediently along with her hand in his, sure that he was equal to any situation that might arise.

For an hour or more the two children wandered about the piazza, carried hither and thither in the wake of the crowds. First they followed the black-cowled Misericordia Brothers as they bore away to the hospital a sick old man who had fallen in the street. Then they found a marionette show and stood entranced for a long time before it, watching the thrilling adventures of Pantalone. After that they crept into the dim Cathedral, now nearly empty of people, and watched the women who came to light their tapers at the Great Paschal Candle beside the altar. It was then that they discovered they were hungry, and, going out on the street, they refreshed themselves with oranges bought of a fruit-vendor.

If Teresina could have seen the children of the Marchesa as they stood sucking oranges in the public street, it is likely she might have fainted with horror, and been carried away to the hospital by the black-robed Brothers of Mercy in her turn; but as it was, Teresina was not there to see. After searching the crowds distractedly for an hour, she had rushed back to the palace, hoping to find the Twins there before her, and turning the whole establishment into an uproar when she found they had not yet appeared.

Meanwhile, the children, unconscious of time, were wandering about enjoying their new freedom, and growing more adventurous at every step. Though they had finished their oranges, they were still hungry, and there was a wonderful smell of roasting chicken in the air, which Beppo followed with the unerring instinct of a hungry boy, and soon the two children were standing before an open cook-shop in a side street, gnawing chicken bones and smacking their lips with as much gusto as if they had been bred in the streets instead of a palace.

When they left the cook-shop, with its rows of bright copper pots and pans and its delicious smells, Beppo had only a few soldi left in his pockets, and as for Beppina, there had been nothing but a handkerchief in hers from the beginning.

"Avanti!" cried Beppo, made more bold than ever by the courage which comes with a full stomach. "Let's explore!" and, seizing the hand of the more timid Beppina, he ventured farther and farther up the narrow street. They had never been in this part of the city before in their lives. They had never even dreamed that people could live in such dark, dirty houses, more like rabbit-warrens than homes for human beings, and on streets so narrow that Beppo could easily leap across them in one jump.

They made their way through groups of idle loungers, stepping cautiously around dirty babies playing in the gutters, and past slatternly mothers gossiping in shrill tones from doorsteps and open windows, quite unconscious of the fact that every one turned to look with astonishment at the strange spectacle of two well-dressed children walking alone through the burrow-like streets of old Florence.

At the opening of a dark passage they almost stumbled over an old woman bent over a charcoal-brazier, where she was roasting chestnuts.

"She looks just like a witch," whispered Beppina, making the devil's horns with her fingers to protect herself from the Evil Eye. "Let's hurry past."

They shrank back against the opposite wall of the narrow passage and tried to squeeze by, but the old woman swept out a bony hand and seized Beppina by the skirt.

"For the love of Santa Maria, just a few soldi, my pretty little lady," she whined, pulling the child toward her. Her smile was so terrifying that Beppina gave a little scream, and with Beppo's help tore herself free of the old woman's grasp. Then the two fled still farther up the street, followed by a storm of abuse and the laughter of the idle people they passed in their flight.

When at last they paused for breath, they found themselves in a labyrinth of narrow alleys, with no idea of which way to turn to get back to the piazza. Beppina was frightened, but Beppo said confidently, "All we've got to do is to keep on going, and we are sure to strike either the piazza or the river, and we shall know how to get home from either one, so don't you be afraid."

Inspired by his boldness, Beppina followed him from one narrow passage to another, until at last the streets began to widen again, and they saw before them an open square, and heard the sound of music. They ran joyously forward and found themselves in a beautiful but strange piazza, with a great fountain playing in the centre, and fine old buildings surrounding it on all sides.

The source of the music was hidden by a throng of people gathered together near the fountain. "It's a hand-organ," cried Beppo eagerly. "Maybe there's a monkey!" and he dashed into the midst of the crowd.

Beppina followed close behind, and the two worked their way under the elbows of the grown people until they reached the very centre, where they were thrilled to find a dark, swarthy man, holding a bear by a rope. The bear was dancing clumsily on his hind legs, and near by a woman with black eyes and hair and great rings in her ears was grinding an organ. On top of the organ sat a monkey in a red cap shaking a tambourine. Behind the group stood a yellow van, drawn by two donkeys gayly tricked out with scarlet nets and jingling bells.

The Twins had no sooner arrived upon the scene than the music stopped, the bear dropped upon all fours, and the monkey, hopping down from the organ, began to leap about among the people, holding out the tambourine for money. Then it was wonderful to see how rapidly the crowd melted away! In a few moments the children were the only ones left. Beppo gave his last coin to the monkey, and the woman, throwing a black look after the disappearing crowd, ground out another tune for them on the organ, while the monkey, to Beppo's great delight, leaped upon his shoulder and searched his pockets with her little black paws.

The man, meanwhile, was preparing to start away. He handed the bear's rope to his wife and, climbing to the driver's seat of the van, cracked his whip, and shouted, "Aiou! aiou! you laggards!" to the donkeys. The monkey leaped from Beppo's shoulder to the back of the bear, and, as the caravan began to move, turned somersaults on the bear's back with such wonderful agility that no boy on earth could have resisted following her. The woman said something to her husband which the children did not understand, though they did not know that it was because she spoke to him in the Venetian dialect; then she turned to Beppo and said with an insinuating smile, "Where is it that the Signore lives?"

Now here was a woman of sense! She called him Signore, as if he were already a grown man! Beppo swelled with satisfaction and answered promptly, "In the Palace Grifoni, across the river."

"Si, si," said the woman, which in Italian means "Yes, yes."

"We are going in that direction. Would you not like to go with us and lead the bear?" Oh, if Teresina could have heard that! Here were people who thought him quite big enough to lead a live bear, while she, and Mammina, too, for that matter, thought he still should be followed by a nurse!

Beppo leaped boldly forward, though Beppina tried to hold him back, and, seizing the bear's rope, marched proudly along behind the van. The woman laughed and clapped her hands. "Bravo, bravo!" she cried. Then, turning to the panic-stricken Beppina, she said comfortingly: "The old Ugolone will not hurt him. He is very old and as tame as a kitten. See!" She gave the bear a slap and walked along beside him with her hand on his back, and Beppina could do nothing but follow.

For some time they trailed the van in this way, together with a small army of boys and girls, who were consumed with envy for Beppo and hoped they too might be allowed a turn at leading the bear. One by one they had dropped away and returned to their homes before the Twins realised that the afternoon was nearly spent and night was approaching.

"We must go home now, please," said Beppina politely to the woman.

"Si, si," said the woman, nodding her head and smiling more than ever. "We shall soon see the river."

This assurance quieted Beppina for a time, and she trudged patiently along until they reached the very outskirts of the city, and still no bridge and no river had appeared. Not Beppina only, but Beppo too now began to be alarmed. Where were they going? Oh, if only the grey walls of the Grifoni palace would rise before them! Beppo even began to modify his opinion about Teresina. Her ruff and streamers would have been as welcome a sight to him just then as an oasis to travellers in the desert. But alas! Teresina was at that moment many miles away, and distracted with anxiety and grief. The bewildered Beppina now began to cry.

"Come, my pretty," said the woman in a wheedling tone, "you are tired, is it not so? You shall rest the weary legs." Her voice was soft, but she seized Beppina with a grip of steel, and swung her up into the back of the moving van. "You too, my brave one," she went on, taking the bear's rope from Beppo's hand, and tying it to a ring in the back of the cart. "Up you go." She gave him a shove as he scrambled up beside Beppina, and then, tossing the monkey in after him, swung herself up beside the children.

The road now began to ascend, and the Twins with growing terror watched the sun sink lower and lower behind the dome of the Cathedral, which they could see in the distance. Beppina shook with sobs, and Beppo sat pale and frightened as the tower and the dome, the only landmarks they knew in Florence, grew darker and darker against the sunset sky.

"Do not cry, madonna mia," said the woman, giving Beppina a little shake. "You have missed your way, but what of that? You are safe with us. If you have money in your pockets you might possibly find your way home even yet, though it is nearly dark, and it is very dangerous for children to go about alone."

"But we haven't any money," said Beppo. "I gave all I had to the monkey!"

"Ah," said the woman, "that is bad, to go back without money! You would spend the night in the streets without doubt, or possibly in the jail. If the police found you they would take you for vagrants. It would be terrible indeed if the police should get you! Still, if you think best you can jump down and start back right now. I do not believe the bear would hurt you, even though he does not like to have any one jump right in front of him!"

The children looked down at Ugolone, lumbering along behind the van. If they jumped it must be almost on top of him, and in the darkness he looked as big as a house and very alarming. Even Beppo lost his swagger, and as for Beppina, she was speechless with terror. The woman continued to cajole them.

"Soon we shall camp beside the road for the night," she said, "and you shall have something hot for your supper, and sleep in the van as cozy as birds in a nest. That is surely much better than the jail! And to-morrow, oh, la bella vita! just think, you shall grind the organ and play with Carina all day long, and there will be no lessons!"

There was no response to this alluring prospect. The children, homesick, weary, terror-stricken, clung to each other in the darkness, and shrank as far as possible from the woman, whom they now saw to be not their friend, but their jailer.

On and on through the deepening darkness lumbered the yellow van, until it seemed to the unhappy children that it must be nearly morning. At last, however, the team turned from the highroad and stopped beside a little stream. The woman sprang out, and while her husband unharnessed the donkeys and tied Ugolone to a tree for the night, she built a fire, and hung a kettle over it. She put the monkey in Beppina's arms, and sent Beppo for water from the stream, and to gather sticks for the fire.

Soon a kettleful of steaming mush was ready, and the woman, whose name was Carlotta, called Luigi, her husband, and, giving the children each a tin dish, bade them eat their supper. Even if it had been her favourite food, Beppina could not have swallowed a mouthful that night, but Beppo, though he too was homesick, could still eat, even though nothing better than polenta was offered him. He sat down with Carlotta and Luigi before the fire on the ground, while Beppina stayed in the back of the van, hugging the monkey to her lonely heart and striving to keep back the tears.

The flickering flames lit up the trunks of the trees, making them stand out like sentinels against the velvet darkness of the woods beyond, and sending dancing shadows of the bear and the donkeys far across the murmuring stream. The moon looked down through the tree-tops and the nightingales sang plaintively in the shadows.

After supper, while Luigi sat smoking his pipe by the fire, Carlotta threw a heap of straw into one corner of the van, and said to the children: "Come hither, my poverelli! Here is a soft bed for you! Lie down and sleep!"

Too tired to do anything else, if, indeed, there had been anything else in the world for them to do, the children obeyed, and, clasped in each other's arms, soon fell asleep, worn-out with sorrow and fatigue.

CHAPTER III. IN THE MOUNTAINS.

They were awakened next morning by the chattering of the monkey, and, looking out from their corner, they could not for a moment remember where they were, or how they came to be there. The sun was shining brightly, the birds were singing, and Carlotta was up and stirring something in a pot over the fire. Luigi had gone with the donkeys to give them a drink, and Ugolone was standing on his hind legs beside his tree, grunting impatiently for his breakfast.

Beppina gazed at the strange scene for one blank moment, then, as memory came back, she buried her head in the straw and sobbed. Beppo tried to comfort her.

"Don't cry, Beppinella," he whispered. "To-day we shall find some way of returning to Florence. I feel sure of it! It might be worse. Pazienza! We must make the best of it."

Just then, Carlotta, hearing the muffled sobs and the murmur of his voice, appeared at the end of the van.

"Come out, little lost ones," she called to them. "The sun shines, and we shall have a fine day in the mountains. See, here is Carina waiting to greet you!" She tossed the monkey toward them as she spoke, and disappeared around the end of the van. Soon she returned, carrying in her hand a green blouse and a gay striped skirt.

"Here," she said to Beppina, "I will lend these to you. Then you can save your pretty clothes so they will be clean to wear when you return to your Mammina." She spoke so confidently of their return that Beppina thought perhaps the woman meant to take them back that very day. She reluctantly put on the queer blouse and the striped skirt, while Beppo arrayed himself in a pair of velveteen trousers which were as much too long for him as the skirt was for Beppina. Carlotta had brought these also, and she gave him a red sash to bind around his waist as well.

When they were equipped in these garments the two children gazed at each other in dismay.

"You don't look like Beppo at all. You look just like a bandit," said Beppina.

"And you, you look like a gypsy girl!" gasped Beppo.

"Even Mammina wouldn't know us if she were to see us now," Beppina whispered, despairingly.

"That's just why that woman did it!" gasped Beppo, with sudden illumination. "She doesn't care a bit about saving our clothes! She wants to disguise us, so people will think we belong to them!"

"Oh, dear!" shuddered Beppina. "Let's change back again."

They seized their clothes, but just then they saw Carlotta's glittering black eyes gazing in at them from the end of the van. It was as if she knew their very thoughts.

"Avanti, avanti!" she called. "Is it that you are lazy? Come! We must be on the road!"

Not daring to linger or protest, the two strange little figures came tumbling out of the straw at once, and, after washing in the brook, sat down on a fallen log to eat their breakfast. Carina perched beside them on the log, and, when she had finished her own portion, leaped on Ugolone's back, and, leaning down, snatched away some of his breakfast from under his nose. In vain poor old Ugolone growled and slapped at her with his clumsy paws. He was always too slow to catch her.

The children were so absorbed in watching this drama that they did not notice what Carlotta was doing meanwhile, but later, when they looked for their own clothes again, they had mysteriously disappeared, and were not seen again.

When they had finished breakfast, Carlotta called to Beppina, "Come here, poverina! Your hair is full of straw. I will fix it for you." Beppina obeyed, and the woman coaxed her tangled locks into place, combing them with her fingers, and at last succeeded in plaiting them into a number of tight braids which she wound about her head. "There," said she when this was done, "now you will no longer need your hat."

"But," said Beppina, "I want my hat! Only peasants go bare-headed."

The woman gave a short laugh, and her teeth gleamed so white between her lips that Beppina thought of the wolf who tried to pass himself off for Red Riding Hood's grandmother.

"Do as you are told," said Carlotta. She smiled as she said it, but there was such a fierce look in her face that Beppina made the sign against the Evil Eye, with her hand behind her, and submitted silently as Carlotta tied a red kerchief over the braids. These preparations completed, the caravan moved on, with Luigi as usual in the driver's seat, Carlotta leading the bear, and the Twins, carrying the monkey, bringing up the rear.

On and on they travelled, but in which direction the children could only guess. There were many turns in the road, which wound constantly upward, and with every mile the country grew more wild. Through openings between the hills they caught fleeting glimpses of quaint villages clinging to the mountain-sides, and of ancient castles commanding beautiful views across fertile valleys. At one time they saw the roofs of a great stone monastery, hidden away among olive trees.

They heard the music of its bells and caught faint echoes of the chanting of the monks. It was then that they remembered that it was Easter Sunday.

"If we were at home, we should now be hunting Easter eggs and sugar lambs in the garden," whispered Beppina.

"Teresina said there wouldn't be any there, anyway," Beppo answered, winking very hard; and then neither one said anything for a long time.

All day long the donkeys plodded up the steep slopes, only stopping by the wayside for rest and food at noon. It was evident that Luigi thought best to keep to the least-frequented mountain ways, so all through the sunny hours the sad little travellers walked behind the van, or climbed inside to rest their weary feet, not knowing where they were going and not daring to ask.

At sunset they reached the crest of a high hill, and, looking back, they could see far, far away in the purple distance, the twinkling lights of the city of Florence, looking like a sky full of stars fallen to earth. On the slopes of nearer hills there were other twinkling lights like chains of jewels winding in and out among the trees. The mountain villages were celebrating the Easter festival with candle-lit processions and with singing. The words of the Easter song floated across the blue spaces. "The Royal Banners forward go," came the faint chant, and, mingling with the vesper song of thrush and nightingale, lulled the tired travellers to dreamless sleep.

CHAPTER IV. THEY LEARN TO DANCE.

It was cold in the mountains, and the children shivered as Carlotta routed them out in the early dawn of the next morning. "Come," she said crossly, as she set up the forked sticks for the kettle, "bestir yourselves, lazy ones! We are poor people. Do you think we can afford to feed you and wait upon you like servants besides? To-day there must be no more snivelling and whining. Beppo, take the pail and fetch water. You, Beppina, gather sticks for the fire."

Her wheedling manner was now quite gone. Instead she gave her orders with such a threatening look that the children trembled with fear as they hastened to obey. At a little distance from the spot where they were encamped, a stream, fed by a mountain spring, gushed forth from a pile of rocks, and Beppo, seizing the pail, plunged into the dark pine woods to find it. Beppina followed, and the instant they found themselves alone in the forest, the two hid behind a tree and held a hurried consultation.

"Listen, cocca mia," whispered Beppo. "I have thought this all out. They do not mean to take us back, ever! They will keep us like slaves to work for them! If we want to see our home again, we must obey everything they say, no matter how hard. Then some day, when they aren't watching, we will run away. Only not in these mountains! We should only die of hunger and be eaten by the wolves."

Beppina shuddered. "Oh, Beppo," she sobbed, "there is a lump in my throat as big as an egg! I cannot swallow it. When I think of Mammina, it seems to me I shall die!"

Beppo gave her a little shake. "But you must be brave," he said. "Every day we will have a word together, and soon our chance will come."

"I'll try, Beppo," said Beppina, gulping down her sobs.

"Good girl!" said Beppo, patting her approvingly, though his own lips trembled and his voice shook. "Don't you remember how it is in the fairy tales? The prince always kills the giants and dragons if only he isn't afraid, even if he has to pass through enchanted forests."

Beppina looked fearfully over her shoulder. "Oh, Beppo," she gasped, "I didn't think of it before, but now I'm sure. This is an enchanted forest, and Carlotta is a witch woman! We must pray always to the Holy Virgin to protect us. Promise me you will!"

"I promise," said Beppo solemnly; "and don't you forget about the prince either."

Just then they heard Carlotta's voice shouting at them, and, leaping apart, they fled to do their errands.

When breakfast had been eaten, and the animals fed, Luigi lit his pipe and stretched out on the ground beside the fire with the monkey beside him.

"Here we stay a little," he said. "Ugolone lies there like one dead. The donkeys are tired and so am I. We have come thirty miles from Florence."

"Ecco!" said Carlotta. "Then there is time for bean soup." She sent Beppo for more water, and, when the kettle was bubbling on the fire, called the children to her side. "Tell me," she said, "can you dance?"

"A little," quavered Beppina. "Dance, then," said the woman. Beppina reluctantly seized her skirts, and, making a dancing-school bow, took a few dainty steps and tripped over a stone.

Carlotta laughed contemptuously. "Santa Maria!" she said, "you don't call that dancing!" Then, beckoning to her husband, she cried, "But they know nothing! They cannot earn their salt! We have made a bad bargain. Come, then, and we will teach these ignorant ones the trescone!"

Luigi grunted as he rose unwillingly from his hard couch, tied the monkey's string about a tree branch, and came forward.

"Watch closely, both of you," said Carlotta to the children. "It is for you to dance like Tuscans, not like marionettes. Even old Ugolone can do better."

Once he was roused, Luigi's weariness seemed to vanish. He suddenly seized Carlotta's hands, and, holding her at arm's length, began to wheel and jump, to turn and twist in all sorts of curious figures.

Sometimes the dancers' arms were linked above their heads. Sometimes they shook a lifted foot. Faster and faster they whirled, and the monkey, inspired by their example, began to leap and bound about at the end of her string, chattering wildly.

The speed of the dancers slackened like that of a spinning top, and they came to a sudden standstill. Luigi returned to Carina and his place by the fire, and Carlotta got out the hand-organ. All the morning she made the children practice the figures of the dance to music, until they were ready to drop with fatigue. While she prepared the soup for their noon meal they were allowed to rest, but immediately afterwards the donkeys were harnessed again, and to the music of their tinkling bells the little cavalcade moved on.

For some time they travelled over the steep mountain roads without seeing a soul; then they met a girl driving a flock of sheep to pasture. Later they overtook some peasant women walking like queens with great loads of wood on their heads. Beyond them they passed an ox-team, and Beppo whispered to Beppina, "It's a good sign to meet oxen in the road."

But alas, a moment later they met a priest, mumbling his prayers as he walked. It was a glance of despair that Beppina gave her brother then, for it is very bad luck to meet a priest in the road, as every Tuscan child can tell you.

Nevertheless, all these signs, bad and good, indicated that they were approaching a town, and a few moments later they came to a stream where women were washing clothes, and the van rumbled across a bridge and into the open square of a small mountain village. In an instant there was great excitement in the town, and all the inhabitants swarmed about the van.

Luigi climbed down from the driver's seat, with Carina on his shoulder, and loosed the bear's rope, while Carlotta brought out the organ, and gave the tambourine to the monkey.

"Balla! Balla!" cried Luigi, and Ugolone rising to his hind legs wearily began his clumsy dance. The children, meanwhile, shrank back out of sight in the van.

"She will make us dance like the bear, I know she will," moaned Beppina, "and I cannot remember the steps!" She crossed herself frantically, and said a prayer to the Virgin, but it was of no avail, for soon Carlotta's wheedling tones reached their hiding-place.

"Avanti, carissimi," she called, and, not daring to disobey or even to linger, the children leaped from the back of the van into the centre of a crowd of round-eyed villagers. The children of the Marchese Grifoni dancing in company with a monkey and a bear for the entertainment of an audience of peasants! The humiliation of it was almost more than they could endure, but the Twins did their best, and the moment the performance was over dived into the back of the van, and hid themselves again, while Carina leaped about among the crowd, gathering the soldi in her tambourine.

Their stay in the village was short, for the people were poor.

"It is a town of pigs," said Carlotta angrily, as she counted the money, and to the great relief of the children she gave the order to move on into the hills beyond the village.

They stopped at one more village during the afternoon, and here things went better. The children remembered their steps, and there were more soldi in the tambourine, even though Ugolone sat firmly down upon his haunches and refused to budge. In vain Luigi tugged at his rope and shouted "Balla! Balla!" It was as if Ugolone, seeing the children dance, had concluded that his dancing days were over, and had resigned in their favour.

To make up for Ugolone the Twins had to dance again and again, and then to their great surprise Carlotta made them sing! They had voices like the whistle of song thrushes in the spring, but how in the world could Carlotta have guessed that? They were too astonished to refuse, even if they had dared, so they opened their mouths and quavered out a song about the swallow, which they had learned in the nursery at home.

This was the song:-

  "Pilgrim swallow, lightly winging,
  Now upon the terrace sitting,
  Ev'ry morn I hear thee singing,
  In sad tones thy song repeating.
  What may be the tale thou'rt telling,
  Pilgrim swallow, near my dwelling?

  "Thou art happier far than I am;
  On free wing at least thou'rt flying
  Over lake and breezy mountain.
  Thou canst fill the air with crying
  His dear name through cave and hollow.
  Thou art free, thou pretty swallow."

It was so familiar a song that all the people joined with them in singing it, and some of them danced to the music of the hand-organ when it played, so that altogether the villagers had a gay time, and as a result Carlotta found many more coins than usual in the tambourine when the performance was over. She glanced triumphantly at her husband as she counted the money. "We have caught two pigeons with one pea after all," she said to him.

"As for that lazy Ugolone, he gets no supper! If he will not work, he shall not eat!"

The children heard and shuddered. "She will treat us like that, too," sobbed Beppina, "and if she's truly a witch she may even turn us into bears!"

Out through sunny vineyards and grey olive orchards beyond the town they followed the winding road, and, as night came on, the weary children saw that they were approaching a ruined castle set high on a spur of the Apennines. The wind swept over the bare hill-top and whistled through the windows of its ruined towers, where hundreds of years before lovely ladies had watched their knights ride forth to battle.

It was a bleak and lonely spot, fit only to be inhabited by ghosts, and Beppina shivered as the wheels of the van rattled over the ancient draw-bridge, and stopped in the overgrown court-yard.

"I know it's enchanted," she whispered to Beppo, and Beppo, his own teeth chattering, could only say, "Remember about the prince," to keep up their failing courage.

There was no sign of human beings about the place, and Luigi took possession as if he owned it. He tied Ugolone in the ruins of what had once been a stately banqueting-hall, and let the donkeys eat their supper from the green grass which carpeted the court-yard.

Soon a fire was blazing in the ruins of an ancient chimney, and the tired travellers gathered about it for their evening meal. From the tower came the surprised hoot of a solitary owl, and bats, disturbed by the light, swooped in great circles about the little group as they silently ate their polenta. Even the monkey seemed to feel the weird spell of the place, for she cowered in a corner by the fire, chattering to herself, while from the banqueting-hall came the complaining growls of poor hungry Ugolone. It was to such music as this that the children of the Marchese at last fell asleep.

CHAPTER V. ON THE ROAD.

When they awoke the next morning Carlotta and Luigi were nowhere in sight. The monkey was tied to one wheel of the van, and from the banqueting-hall came the sound of human voices, quarrelling. The tones were so loud that the children could not help hearing the words.

"It is all your fault!" said Luigi's voice. "It was you who made me get the bear in the first place, and undertake this foolish trip, all because you must again see your people in Florence. If we had but stayed in Venice! The bear was old when we got him; he was already tired and sick when we left Florence, and now, per Bacco, he is dead! You would not feed him, yet it was Ugolone that we depended upon to bring in the money. A hand-organ, a monkey, what are they? And now you have added those brats beside for us to feed! This comes of listening to a woman and a smooth-tongued Tuscan at that. I could beat you!"

Carlotta's wheedling voice answered him. "Do not grieve, my angel," she said; "you will yet see the wisdom of your Carlotta. Ugolone was old and sick, it is true. A pest upon the villain who sold him to us! May his eyes weep rivers of tears! But you are wrong about the children. They are worth more than Ugolone, the donkeys, and the van, all put together. Did you not see how they pleased the people yesterday? I will teach them to sing more songs, and to dance the tarantella as well as the trescone, and we shall soon forget this sorrow. When we reach the coast, we will sell the van and the donkeys, and go back to your beloved Venice, to live in comfort on the earnings of these brats! You shall see!"

"That's more of your oily Tuscan talk," growled Luigi. "Think of the risk we run! If the ragazzini should be recognised, it would go hard with us. Their parents will lay every trap to catch us. It is safe enough in these mountain villages, but in the larger towns it will be a different story. There are the police -"

Carlotta interrupted him. "Che, che!" she cried. "You have the heart of a chicken! I tell you, even their own mother would hardly know them now, and it will be easy to hide them in Venice. We shall be like rats in the walls of a house, where the cat cannot follow. As for traps, we are too sharp for them. Even if we were to be seen and tracked, they will not seek donkeys and a van in Venice, where there are no such things."

Luigi only grunted for reply, and Carlotta, seeing that her arguments had made an impression, boldly finished her plan.

"When we reach the coast," she said, "you remain behind to sell the van, and I will go on to Venice with the ragazzini. We shall not be pursued upon the boat. Courage! In a few days we shall be safe, and then we can live at ease, and you will say, `Ah, what a great head has my Carlotta!'"

There was no reply from Luigi, and soon the children heard their returning footfalls on the stone flagging.

"Pretend you're asleep," whispered Beppo. "We mustn't let them think we overheard." They instantly lay down in the straw again, and when Carlotta came to the back of the van a moment later, she was obliged to call twice before she could arouse them!

While Carlotta, looking very glum, was cooking the everlasting polenta, the children crept fearsomely into the ruined tower to take a last look at poor old Ugolone. There he lay on the flag-stones, a shapeless lump of fur, and a little later Luigi skinned him, hung the pelt on the back of the van, and, leaving the bones to whiten where they lay, set forth once more upon the road. From this time on things grew harder and harder for the unhappy children. Carlotta was caressing and smooth in her manner to them when they were in the villages, calling them "my children," "carissimi," which means "dearest," and other tender names, but when they were by themselves she grew more and more harsh, while Luigi was sullen, and scarcely spoke to them at all.

It was Carlotta who made them dance until they were ready to drop with fatigue, and sing when their hearts were breaking. Everywhere the people thought them charming, and it was true, as Carlotta had said, that they brought in more money than Ugolone.

They were now passing through one of the most lovely regions in the world, but its beauty failed to comfort them or reconcile them to their lot. The rocky ramparts and blue horizon of the mountains were but prison walls to them, from which they longed to escape. One night, as they lay shivering in the straw, with Carlotta and Luigi snoring at the other end of the van, Beppo cautiously nudged his sister.

"It sounds like Teresina," he whispered. "Don't you remember how she snored that day we left home?"

"Don't," begged Beppina. "It makes me homesick."

"I never thought I could wish to hear Teresina snore," Beppo answered, "but now it would be music in my ears." They were silent a few minutes, and then Beppina, timid Beppina, put her lips close to Beppo's ear and whispered, "Let's get out and run away."

"Where to?" Beppo whispered.

"Anywhere, anywhere away from here!" said poor Beppina. "I'd rather starve in the mountains than stay any longer. We could creep out without waking them."

"It's awfully dark," said Beppo, "and we'll have to climb right over them!"

"Oh, let's try," urged Beppina. They sat up cautiously and peered out. They could just see a dark mass blocking up the open end of the van. They struggled to their knees. The straw rustled, and they stopped dead, until everything was still again. Then Beppo rose to his feet, and, treading very carefully, took a step toward the end of the van.

But alas, he had forgotten the monkey! She slept beside her mistress, and Beppo stepped on her tail! There was a scream as Carina leaped up in the air, and lit on Beppo's shoulder, chattering furiously, and Beppo instantly dropped down into the straw again.

"What's the matter?" said Carlotta.

The children could see her dark silhouette as she sat up and looked into the dark interior of the van.

"Carina mia! What is the matter?"

"Lie down," growled Luigi. "She has had a bad dream. Go to sleep!" The monkey leaped to Carlotta's arm, snuggled down beside her, and quiet reigned once more. When the snores began again, the children had no courage for a second attempt, and morning found things as hopeless as ever.

They were now descending the eastern slopes of the Apennines, and Beppo, remembering his geography, knew that they were getting farther and farther from Florence. At noon that day, as they were walking ahead of the van, they rounded a turn in the road, and came suddenly upon a view stretching far across the plains of eastern Italy to where the blue waters of the Adriatic lay sparkling in the sun. The landscape was dotted with villages, and far away in the blue distance they could see the spires and towers of a large coast town.

Beppo's spirits rose a little. "See," he said to Beppina, "we are coming out of the mountains into a region where there are many towns. Who knows? Perhaps we may find a chance to get away. It would be less dangerous here than in the hills."

But again they were doomed to disappointment, for the next day it rained, and Carlotta made them stay hidden in the van as it lumbered slowly through the villages on the road to the sea. Though it was only two days, it seemed at least a week that they lay in the straw, listening to the rumble of the wheels and the patter of the rain on the roof. There could be no fires, so their food was bread and cheese, which Carlotta bought in the towns.

At last, early on the third morning, they heard from their prison a new sound, and, peering cautiously over Luigi's shoulder, saw that at last they had reached the sea. They could hear the slapping of waves against the piles of a dock, and could catch glimpses of green water. Men with trucks were hurrying by, loading fruit and vegetables upon a large boat which was tied to the pier. There was so much noise about them that the children could talk together in low tones without being overheard.

"I know where we are," said Beppo. "I tell you, I'm glad I studied geography! The sun is breaking through the clouds over the water, and it's early morning, so that's the east, of course. We heard Carlotta say they were going to take us to Venice, so this must be a coast town on the Adriatic. It isn't Ravenna, because Ravenna is back from the sea a few miles. The only other big port along here is Rimini, and I'll bet that's just where we are."

"Oh, Beppo, what a wonderful boy you are, to think that all out yourself!" said Beppina. "You're such a wonderful thinker! Why can't you think of a way to escape?"

"I do think, all the time," answered poor Beppo, "but Carlotta is just like a cat at a mouse-hole. Her eyes never leave us, and if we should try to run, she would pounce -"

"Hush!" whispered Beppina, "there she is." There, indeed, she was, smiling craftily at them from the end of the van.

"You may come out now, my little ones," she said in her most syrupy tones. "Here we leave the van with Luigi, while we take a nice boat-ride!" She seized them firmly by the hands, and, followed by Luigi carrying the organ and the monkey, led them over the gang-plank on to the boat. Once aboard, she sought an obscure corner, behind the baskets of fruit and vegetables with which the vessel was loaded, and made the children sit beside her, while Luigi piled around them numerous bundles brought from the van.

At last the rumble of trucks ceased, the sailors loosed the great hawsers which tied the boat to the dock, and in a few moments the children, looking back to the shore, saw a widening strip of green water between them and their native land.

CHAPTER VI. VENICE.

For two beautiful bright days they remained on the boat, as it made its way up the eastern coast of Italy, and on the morning of the third, there, rising before them out of the mists, like a dream city afloat upon the waters, was Venice! It was so lovely, with its domes, towers, and palaces mirrored in the still waters, and its hundreds of sails making spots of bright colour against the blue, that for a short time the children almost forgot their grief. As the boat entered a great lagoon, and slowly made its way through the Canal della Giudecca to the landing-place, Carlotta grew more than ever vigilant. The children had hoped against hope that some way of escape might appear when they reached the dock, but Carlotta remained at their elbows every moment, and under her watchful eyes they could not even speak to each other, much less to any one else.

It was evident that she meant to make them understand how impossible it would be for them to get away from Venice, for as the boat rounded the western side of the island upon which the city is built, she pointed out to them the mainland, lying two miles away across the water, and the long black railroad bridge which is the only connection between the two.

"You see how it is, my little ones," she said. "One cannot leave Venice without a boat, a ticket on the railway, or wings! And truly, how could any one wish to leave it? Luigi has been wretched all the time he has been away, and never wishes to desert his beloved city again. You too will feel the same."

The children made no reply. They were as helpless as caged birds, and could only follow her silently, as she loaded them with bundles, and, herself carrying the organ and the monkey, led the way across the gang-plank to the dock. Staggering under their burdens, they entered the city of Venice. Oh, if they could only have entered it with their dear Babbo, or Mammina, how happy they would have been, for there, right before their eyes as they walked, were all the wonderful things which Beppo had learned about in his geography!

There were the canals with the gondolas flitting about on them like black beetles on a pool. There were the great beautiful buildings with their facades rising out of the water, and their back doors opening upon narrow streets or tiny open squares. There were the glimpses of blossoming tree-tops hanging over high walls, and of balconies gay with potted geraniums and carnations in bloom. There were the beautiful stone door-ways with gayly painted posts beside them, to which empty gondolas were tied.

The air was misty and fragrant with sea smells, and in every direction they looked their eyes were greeted with the lovely colours of the old buildings, reflected in the water so clearly that it seemed as if there were two cities, one hanging suspended upside down below the other. It was so different from Florence, from Rome, from anything they had ever seen before, that the children forgot even that they were hungry, and went up the streets wide-eyed with wonder, absorbed in all these marvels.

"Get on, get on!" said Carlotta crossly, behind them. "Your eyes will pop out of your heads, and drop in the street if you stare so. Carina is hungry, and so am I, and we must earn our dinner before we eat it."

Through one narrow street after another they made their way, until at last they reached an open square fronting on the water.

"Here is the market," said Carlotta, depositing the organ in the middle of the open space, and the children, sighing with relief, also dropped their bundles and gazed about them. Drawn up to the water's edge were many boats loaded with great baskets of fruit and vegetables. Merchants swarmed about these boats like flies, and the produce was immediately purchased and placed in stalls or booths around the edge of the square, where people with market-baskets on their arms were buying their provisions for the day.

It was a busy and crowded place, but Carlotta gave the children little time to look. "Dance," she commanded, as she began to grind out a tune upon the organ. Carina sprang to the top of the box, and began to hop up and down in time to the music as the children went through the wild contortions of the trescone. A crowd immediately gathered about them, and the coins began to rain into Carina's tambourine.

When the dance was finished, Carlotta led the way to a booth in the square, where hot macaroni was for sale, and here their hungry mouths were filled with the first warm food they had tasted for several days. They ate and were comforted. Then, leaving the market-place, they passed through narrow streets and over little bridges spanning the canals, until they reached another small open square in a crowded portion of the city. Carlotta walked faster and faster as they approached it, and the Twins had almost to run to keep up with her.

As they entered the square, a small dirty boy about Beppo's size suddenly gave a shout. "It is Carina!" he cried, and, not noticing Carlotta or the Twins, he seized the monkey in his arms and kissed its little black face. Carlotta gave him a playful slap.

"Ecco!" she cried to the Twins. "Here we have the brave Giovanni! And he cares nothing for his godmother! He loves only the little black monkey! See, Giovanni! I have brought two playmates for you. They were lost, and I have protected them out of charity. They will live with us."

Giovanni stared at the Twins for a moment, then he ran out his tongue at Beppo. "I can lick you!" he cried. Beppo stiffened with fury. All the pent-up rage of the past weeks rose up within him, and here was some one on whom he could legitimately wreak it! He dropped his bundles, rolled up his sleeves, and roared, "Come on!"

Giovanni threw the monkey at Carlotta and instantly came on! A crowd of ragged boys and girls gathered about them, and the fight began. It did not last long, for Beppo had taken boxing-lessons along with his other studies, and he met Giovanni's advance with a swift blow which sent him spinning to the ground. Then he sat upon him until he begged for mercy, while the crowd squealed with delight. Carlotta turned the organ and the monkey over to Beppina, picked Beppo off the prostrate Giovanni, and then, seizing the two boys by their collars, thumped their heads smartly together.

"Ecco!" she said. "Now you have had your fight, you can be friends." Loading them both with bundles, she marched them across the square to the back door of a dilapidated house, with the crowd surging about them. Here she drew them into a narrow entrance and, leading them up two flights of dirty stairs, knocked at a door. It was opened by a slatternly woman, who gave a shrill cry of astonishment when she saw the group on her threshold.

The monkey evidently knew her, for he leaped from Giovanni's arms to her shoulder and began to pull her hair.

"Santa Maria! Santa Maria!" screamed the woman. "If it is not that devil of a Carina come back again! Let go of my hair, you demon, or I'll wring your black neck!"

Carlotta laughed, and picked the monkey off of Giovanni's mother just as she had picked Beppo off of her son a few moments before.

The children, left to themselves, stared about at their new quarters, while Giovanni stared at them. The room was large, bare, dilapidated, and dirty. On the floor were some old mattresses filled with corn-husks, which were evidently used as beds. There was a wooden table with some soiled dishes standing on it, and, beyond this and a few chairs, there was no furniture except two pots of geraniums on the window-sill. A door opened into a smaller room beyond, and through it they could see a stove, with a kettle standing on the floor beside it.

Giovanni had evidently made up his mind that any one who could "lick" him must indeed be a hero, for, having finished his critical survey of the Twins, he said affably, "My father is a gondolier. What's yours?"

"A Marchese," said Beppo.

"Holy Madonna!" gasped the boy. "Doesn't he do any work?"

"No," said Beppo. "He just goes to Rome to help the King."

Carlotta overheard them. "Don't you ever say that again, you wicked little liar!" she cried fiercely. "If you do, I'll cut off your tongue." She turned again to the other woman.

"Do they look like the children of a Marchese? I ask you," she said. "They were lost, and I have taken care of them out of charity! They sing and dance to pay for their keep, but it's little enough they bring in at best! Old Ugolone is dead, and Luigi has stayed behind to dispose of the van and the donkeys. With the money he gets for them he'll buy a boat and pick up a living on the canals. We shall go no more on tours about the country. It does not pay. There are as many soldi to be found in Venice as anywhere, and with the organ and Carina we shall get along, even with two extra mouths to feed!"

Giovanni's mother winked her eye and nodded a great many times.

"Si, si," she said. "There will be many tourists in Venice this summer, and it is not to believe the way Americans throw money about. Mario says their pockets are lined with gold!"

Sick with terror, the children turned away from Carlotta and looked out of the windows.

"See me," said Giovanni. He wanted to do something to make himself admired after his recent humiliation, so he doubled himself across the sill of the open window and leaned far out over the canal which flowed directly beneath. "Look!" he cried, waving his legs at the peril of taking a header into the water.

His mother seized him. "Madonna mia," she screamed, "that boy would rather drown than not," and, giving him a smart spank, she jerked him back into the room by a leg. Giovanni rubbed the spot and grinned sheepishly, as his mother followed up the punishment by a flow of speech which sounded to the Twins much like the chattering of the monkey. "Get along with you!" she said finally, giving him a shove.

"Come," said Carlotta to the Twins when this little scene was over. "Soldi grow only in the street," and, picking up the organ, she led the way down the stairs.

The children were glad to follow, for they preferred the streets to such a dwelling, and Giovanni, thinking it advisable to remain out of his mother's sight for a while, followed them, carrying the monkey in his arms.

CHAPTER VII. THREE WEEKS DRIFT BY.

All the rest of that day, and for many days after, the children followed Carlotta through the maze of streets, dancing and singing in the piazzas and the market-place, or anywhere else where crowds were gathered. Giovanni, having nothing else to do, went with them much of the time, and added his talents to the exhibition. He could turn "cart-wheels" until he looked like a real whirling wheel with only four spokes, and he could walk on his hands. He was glad to display these accomplishments, for he liked being away from home, he liked Carina, and best of all he liked the Twins. The three became quite friendly, and Carlotta, seeing this, smiled her sly smile, and winked knowingly at Giovanni's mother, as though to say: "You see, they are getting used to their new way of living. Soon they will forget their old home, and I shall have no more trouble with them."

Little by little the children came to know Venice better than they had known Florence, which is not saying much, since in Florence they had so completely lost themselves. They could go from Giovanni's house to the Rialto, the largest of the three bridges which span the Grand Canal, and find their way through the maze of streets to the beautiful Piazza of San Marco. They liked best to go there, not only because it is the most beautiful spot in Venice, not even because it is said to be the finest piazza in the world, but also because the flocks of pigeons flying about in clouds, and lighting upon their shoulders, made them think of their own little garden in Florence.

Carlotta liked the piazza because it was the best place in Venice to gather in the soldi. There were always tourists in the square, walking about with guide-books in their hands, and reading passages about its history aloud to one another. Indeed, there was no end to the wonderful things in that famous square. There was the Church of San Marco itself, with its beautiful mosaics and the four splendid bronze horses over the entrance. There was the magnificent Ducal Palace, packed full of thrilling stories of past splendour; and, back of it, spanning the canal, the "Bridge of Sighs," which led from the palace to a dark prison on the other side. On the day she first saw that, Beppina shed tears, thinking of all the unhappy prisoners who had passed over the bridge never to return. She knew how prisoners felt.

Giovanni tried to comfort her. "Don't you fret about them," he said. "They're as dead as they can be, all of 'em, and in purgatory or a worse place, and you can't get 'em out no matter how hard you pray. Come on; let's go look at the clock."

Beppina knew that Carlotta would be angry if they lingered, but still she crossed herself and murmured a hurried "Our Father" for the poor prisoners, on the chance of its helping them, before she ran back to Beppo and Giovanni. She found them standing before the great clock-tower which rose above a high gateway over the street. It was almost noon, and a crowd had gathered to see the clock strike the hour.

There was always a group waiting there on the hour, for this was no ordinary clock. The children watched with breathless interest as two bronze giants on the platform high above their heads suddenly lifted their arms and struck a huge bell twelve times, then relapsed into bronze statues again. Giovanni told the Twins that at Christmas-time the Three Wise Men came out of the clock and bowed before the Madonna and Child. The Twins thought this could be nothing else than a miracle, but Giovanni, who was wise beyond his years, said it was just works in the clock's insides. "It's no more a miracle than a stomach-ache inside of you," he explained.

There was no time for further revelations on the day this happened, for at that moment Carlotta called them. She was afraid the crowd would disperse before she had coaxed money from their pockets. Every moment that they were not dancing or singing, the children wandered about this magic place, where in every direction they looked there were wonderful stories in bronze, marble, or mosaic. One could stay there a year and not begin to know them all. If it rained, they took refuge under the arcade of the Ducal Palace or in the quiet interior of the Church of San Marco itself. Sometimes they could even step in and pray before the altar. Their prayers were always the same, that the Holy Virgin and Saint Anthony, the special guide of those who were lost, would take care of them and bring them safely again to their Babbo and Mammina and their lovely home.

Many days passed in this way, and it was the middle of May before the children ever rode in a boat, for though Giovanni's father had a gondola, it was his business to take passengers about Venice just like a cab-driver in our own cities, and he did not use it for pleasure rides for Giovanni and his friends.

Then one afternoon when they returned from singing in the piazza, they found Luigi waiting to show Carlotta the boat which he had bought with the money he received for the donkeys and the van. It was not a gondola, but a sandalo, a large row-boat, with a pair of oars, suited to carry either passengers or freight.

"The weather is warm now," said Luigi to Carlotta; "the tourists are already lingering on the canals for pleasure in the evenings, and I believe we should do well to let the children go about with me in the boat to sing."

Though they were weary from dancing and singing all day in the streets, it would be far pleasanter to drift about on the canal in the evening than to spend it tossing about on the husk mattresses in Giovanni's squalid house, and the children listened with eager attention to Carlotta's reply.

"As you like," she said, shrugging her shoulders; and that very evening the plan was carried out. Luigi rowed the boat slowly about on the Grand Canal, and the sweet voices of the children, floating out over the still waters, attracted the gondolas about them, and many soldi were flung to the singers.

As the weather grew warmer, the evenings on the canal grew longer and longer. Sometimes the gondolas would join together in long chains and float about in the moonlight with every one joining in the singing. On festival nights there were Chinese lanterns in every prow, and the boats, flitting about over the water, looked like giant fireflies at play.

In this way three weeks drifted by, and at last it was June, and still the children had made no progress toward freedom.

CHAPTER VIII. BEPPO HAS A PLAN.

One day, when they had just finished a performance in the piazza and were allowed to wander for a few moments by themselves, Beppo drew Beppina to the water's edge, and, looking up at the winged lion of Saint Mark's, said to her, "Do you remember what Carlotta said about having to have a boat, a railroad ticket, or wings to get out of Venice?"

Beppina remembered very well.

"The wings on that lion made me think of it," said Beppo, "and I've thought of something else too. There's another thing you need, and that's brains! I've got those, and I'm going to get out of this water-soaked old place or die in the attempt!"

"Oh, Beppo," breathed Beppina, "how?"

"I've got it all planned," said Beppo.

"I guess Saint Anthony must have put it into your head," sighed Beppina, "for he takes care of all the lost people. Anyway, you haven't thought of anything before."

"I thought of this my own self," said Beppo, rather resentfully.

"Well," said Beppina, clasping her hands, "you think, and I'll pray. I'm going to begin a novena. I'll pray hard to Saint Anthony every day for nine days, and ask him to please, please guide us! I'm going to begin right now." She crossed herself and began moving her lips in prayer, but got no farther than "Blessed Saint Anthony," when Beppo nudged her with his elbow.

"Stop it!" he whispered, "here comes the old cat." (He meant Carlotta.) "Don't you let her catch you praying to Saint Anthony, or she'll know what we're up to. You can pray like fury, but say your prayers in your heart, and then some night if I wake you up, you just keep as still as a mouse and follow me."

Carlotta reached them just then and ordered them to go with her back to the Cathedral to sing, and all that day there was no chance for Beppo to explain his great idea. Beppina caught him many times with his forehead all snarled up as if he were trying to think how much 9 times 7 was, or something hard like that, but just what he had in mind she could not guess.

That night when they were out in the boat, Beppo asked Luigi if he might try to row it home, and Luigi, being willing to loaf whenever it was possible, said he might. Beppo did so well that night that on the next Luigi allowed him to row as well as sing, and very soon Beppo came to know his way about the Grand Canal better than he knew the multiplication-table, oh, much better!

At last one night, after they had gone to bed, Beppo lay still for a long time, until he was sure that every one else in the room was asleep. Then he quietly woke Beppina, and the two slid from their mattresses to the floor. Here they waited a moment, for the husks rattled a little, and then, as no one stirred, they moved stealthily to the door, carrying their shoes in their hands. They had slept in their clothes, for they still wore the ones Carlotta had given them, and had not seen their own since the day she had made them change in the van.

They almost suffocated with fright as they opened the door, for it creaked and they feared the monkey would begin to chatter, but Carina was tired, too, and slept as soundly as the rest. In a moment they had quietly closed it behind them, and were feeling their way in the dark, down the stairs and through the passage at the bottom to the canal entrance of the house, where Mario and Luigi kept their oars. Beppo had noted carefully when they came in just where Luigi had placed his, and, feeling cautiously along the wall with his hands, was able to locate them in the dark. He gave his shoes to his sister, took down the oars, and managed to get them to the door without knocking anything over or dropping them on the stone floor.

Followed by Beppina, who was holding on to his coat and praying to Saint Anthony under her breath, he reached the water entrance to the house, and stood upon the landing. Luigi's boat and Mario's gondola were both tied to a red pole beside the entrance. Beppo put one oar down on the step, and with the other managed to reach the pointed prow of the boat, and draw it to the step. Then he leaped in, helped Beppina in with the shoes, took the other oar into the boat with him, and, untying the rope which fastened it to the pole, shot out into the stream.

There was a scraping noise as the boat swung against the landing-step, and Beppo used the oar to push it away. There was also the rattling of the oar-locks, as he backed round and glided out into the canal, but though he was nearly dead with excitement and fright, Beppo kept his head. Never had he managed the boat so well. It slid through the water like a fish. They had gone two or three hundred feet and reached the point where the smaller waterway opened into the Grand Canal, when Beppina was appalled to see the dim outline of another boat a little distance behind them. "They're following!" she gasped. "Oh, Beppo, hurry!"

Beppo bent to his oars and the boat fairly shot through the water! On and on they sped, past the great palaces now dark and grim in starlight, past the market-place, round the great curve of the canal, and soon to their great relief the black boat was no longer following.

"Do you suppose it was Luigi?" gasped Beppina.

"No," said Beppo, "he couldn't possibly have got after us so quickly, because I untied Mario's gondola too. It would drift away far enough so Luigi would have to swim to get it, and he couldn't do it in this time, I know. Maybe it was a police boat, or maybe it was some one going home late. Anyway, he wasn't after us, so I don't care who he was."

"Oh, Beppo, tell me your plan. Where are we going?" begged Beppina.

"Keep still," growled Beppo; "the less noise we make the more chance there is of our getting away."

Beppina crumpled up in the bottom and said no more, while Beppo made the boat skim on over the dark waters. At last he turned the prow toward shore and touched at a dock where many boats were already moored. There was no sign of life about the place, as they disembarked. There was only the soft lapping of the water to break the silence.

"Stoop down," whispered Beppo. "These are the boats that cross over to Mestre on the mainland before daylight to bring fruit and vegetables back to market, and it may be that some of the men sleep in the boats. We might wake them."

For a few moments they listened, crouching down on the dock, and then, as they heard no sound, Beppo gave the sandalo a shove away from shore, and let go the rope.

"Oh," whispered Beppina, "why did you do that?"

"We don't want it any more," answered Beppo, "and if they find it, they'll think we fell out and were drowned. Then they won't look for us."

"Oh, Beppo," said Beppina, "what a wonderful boy you are!"

"I've been planning this a long time," Beppo answered, with a little of his old swagger; "but we aren't out of our troubles yet."

They crept along the dock on their hands and knees until they came to one of the largest flat-bottomed boats in the fleet. Here Beppo paused, and, after carefully examining to be sure it was the one he was looking for, he helped Beppina aboard, and climbed in after her. There was a pile of empty baskets and boxes at one end of the boat, and behind these the children hid themselves to wait for dawn. For a long time they crouched there, listening to the thumping of their own hearts, and the lap-lap-lapping of the water, and at last, completely exhausted with fatigue and fright, curled up on the floor of the boat and fell sound asleep.

CHAPTER IX. THE ESCAPE.

Beppo awoke next morning in the early dawn, and, forgetting where he was, stretched his cramped legs. In doing so he kicked over a basket, which fell on Beppina. Beppina instantly sat up, and, blinking with sleep, said quite loudly, "Where are we?" She might well ask, for there, directly in front of her, pulling stoutly at a pair of oars, sat a short, thick-set man with brown skin and rings in his ears. The level rays of the sun, just rising over Venice, shone full upon his weather-beaten face and astonished eyes, as he gazed at the apparition before him. Just then Beppo's head appeared beside his sister's, and the man, overcome with astonishment, "caught a crab" and splashed both children with water before he burst into speech.

"Madonna mia!" he cried, "am I bewitched? How in the name of all the saints in paradise did you get into this boat? You weren't in it when I left the dock!"

"Oh, yes, we were," said Beppo. "We were behind the baskets."

"But what are you here for?" demanded the man.

"We want to go to Mestre," said Beppo.

The man regarded them suspiciously. "Do your folks know where you are?" he asked.

"No," said Beppo. "That's why we are here. We want to get back to them."

Beppina interrupted. "We were stolen away by gypsies," she said.

Then, still staring at them, the man asked, "Where are you from?"

"From Florence," Beppo answered.

The man threw back his head and laughed. "That's a likely story!" he roared. "From Florence! Ha, Ha! Very good, per Bacco! You are indeed clever liars! You are a pair of naughty little runaways, that's what you are, and if I had time I'd take you straight back to Venice now! As it is, I'll wait until I get my load, and then back you go, and I hope you'll get a good spanking into the bargain."

The children said nothing. They couldn't; they were crushed. But during the rest of the journey Beppo thought as he had never thought in his life before, while Beppina prayed fervently under her breath. During the weeks that they had been so closely watched by Carlotta, Beppina had grown almost to read Beppo's thoughts, so when he furtively took her hand, lifted one eyebrow, and jerked his head in the direction of Mestre, she knew he meant to try to go forward no matter what happened.

They were now nearly across the lagoon and approaching the harbour. Early as it was, the water was already swarming with craft of all descriptions, for Venice has to get all her supplies from the mainland, and many boats are required for the traffic. There was consequently a great deal of shouting back and forth as the men jockeyed for the best positions at the dock. Their own brown boatman was so busy bawling at his competitors and shunting about that for a few moments he was unable to pay any attention to the children. At last, however, he crowded in between two other boats, and while he was explaining to their owners that they were the sons of pigs to take up so much room, Beppo seized his sister by the arm, and the two leaped into the next boat, from that to a third, and then to the dock; and before their captor realised they were gone, they were already speeding frantically up the dock.

"Stop them! Stop them!" howled the boatman, climbing out and starting in pursuit.

Two or three other men joined him, shouting, "Stop! Stop!" too, but their calls only lent speed to the flying feet of the runaways. They did not know where they were going, but they ran as rabbits run when the dogs are after them, and soon found themselves in the streets of the town. The cries of their pursuers grew fainter, and were lost altogether as Beppo suddenly dashed into a side street and they doubled on their tracks.

From a safe hiding-place behind an old building in an alley they caught a glimpse of their pursuers as they turned back to the boats, talking volubly and gesticulating like windmills. They were telling the boatman who had brought the children over what they thought of him for getting them into such a wild-goose chase. Beppo actually chuckled as he watched them go, so great was his relief.

"Now, Beppina," he said, almost gayly, "we'll hurry to the other end of the town as fast as we can go, and get something to eat. I've got ten soldi in my pocket that I picked up when Luigi wasn't looking, and I'm as hungry as a bear. They won't follow us any more, but we'll keep out of sight until the shops are open, anyway."

For an hour or more they wandered quietly about, through the by-ways of the town, until they found a small bake-shop on an unfrequented street; and when an old woman appeared and took down the shutters, they went in and boldly asked for bread and cheese. The woman eyed them with some curiosity, but asked no questions, and they got out as quickly as possible and hid behind an empty house on the outskirts of the village to eat their breakfast.

"I'm sure of one thing," said Beppo, as he munched his bread. "I'm not going to tell our story to any one after this. People would only think we were lying. We'll find our own way to the villa, and earn our money as we go along. Padua is only about thirty miles from here, anyway."

"Oh, Beppo," said Beppina, much impressed, "how did you know that?"

"Geography," said Beppo proudly. "You remember how I knew about Ravenna and Rimini, and, besides, the other day I asked a tourist to let me see the map in the guidebook. Padua is almost straight west from here. We can go away from the sun in the morning and toward it in the afternoon, and we can't help running into it. We'll dance in the villages as we go along, and when we get to Padua it will be easy enough to find the villa."

Beppina had some secret doubts. She remembered how sure Beppo was about finding his way in Florence, but she didn't say a word. She was willing to take any risk if only they could keep out of the clutches of Carlotta.

"Do you suppose they are hunting for us in Venice?" she asked.

"I shouldn't wonder," answered her brother, glancing at the sun. Then he chuckled, "I'll bet they're mad! I hope they'll never find their old boats!"

"Let's get away from here as fast as we can," urged Beppina. "They might follow us, or they might send word to the police."

"That's true," said Beppo. "We can't be too careful."

They had finished their breakfast by this time, and, taking their direction from the sun, set forth at once toward the west. Soon they were out among the suburbs. Then they passed stately villas owned by wealthy Venetians, and beyond that came into open country. It was much easier walking than it had been in the mountains, for the land was level, or gently rolling, the villages were near together, and the highways well travelled. Moreover, they had been hardened to much walking by their weeks of constant practice, and were able to trot along the road at a good rate of speed.

At noon they reached a village, and here they decided to replenish their little hoard of money, so, making their way to the piazza, they surrounded themselves with a crowd for whom they danced the trescone and sang themselves hoarse. They were just gathering up the few coins that were thrown to them, when Beppo saw a policeman approaching, and, not wishing to take any chances, the two children instantly disappeared like smoke down a side street, and out into the highway once more.

By supper-time they had covered ten miles, and when night overtook them, they were in open farming country, surrounded by olive orchards, vineyards, and cornfields. In a field beside the road they came upon a straw-stack, and, hiding themselves on the farther side of it, they ate the bread and ham which they had bought on the way, and then, pulling the straw down over them for covering, slept peacefully until morning.

CHAPTER X. HOME AGAIN.

The next day and the next passed in much the same way. They danced and sang in the villages to earn their bread, and then passed out again to the highway, where there were sign-posts to guide them, or they could ask directions from fellow travellers. One night they passed in an olive orchard, under a spreading tree. Another was spent under the protection of a wayside shrine.

When he awoke in the morning, Beppo found his sister kneeling before the shrine. She turned a beaming face upon him as he opened his eyes.

"Oh, Beppo mio," she said, "I haven't forgotten once, and this is the ninth day! I've made my novena! I'm almost sure the blessed Saint Anthony means to get us to Padua this very day. If he does, I think I shall die of joy."

"What would be the good of that?" Beppo inquired, practically. Then he added, "Anyway, I think it'll be very mean if he doesn't, after all the praying you've done, and all my thinking too."

They ate a hasty bite of bread beside the shrine, then trudged on, and, before the morning was over, actually found themselves passing through the beautiful gardens which surround the city of Padua. They entered it from the east by the Porta di' Pontecorbo, walked a short distance along a wide street, crossed a canal, and, turning to the left, saw rising before them from a great open piazza the huge church of Saint Anthony of Padua, crowned by its six domes and many spires. It was as if they had known every inch of the way, so directly had they come.

The bells of the church were pealing joyfully, and the square was full of people, all going toward the church, for it was the festa of Saint Anthony, though the children did not know it.

Passers-by glanced curiously at the two queer, forlorn little figures, but no one spoke to them, and they stood for a moment uncertain what to do, or in what direction to go, when suddenly Beppina gave a shriek of joy, and, springing forward, threw her arms about a tall, stern-looking woman in a nurse's ruff and streamers who was hurrying toward the church carrying an immense loaf of bread in her hand.

"Teresina!" screamed Beppina.

The woman looked at the child in blank astonishment, but it was not until she saw Beppo that the light of recognition dawned in her face. Then, dropping the bread and falling upon her knees, she engulfed both ragged, dirty children in a wide embrace.

"Oh, thanks be to God, the blessed Virgin, and Saint Anthony, you are found again!" she cried, her eyes streaming tears and her tongue prayers of thanksgiving at the same time. "I was just on my way to offer this bread at the shrine of the blessed Saint, and pray, as I have prayed daily since you were lost, that you might be found again! And here before I have even been to the church at all, the blessed Saint has heard my prayers, and you rise up before me as if out of the ground. It is a miracle! Ah, Madonna mia! what tears the Signora has wept for you! And the Signore your father, he has not slept for seeking you! Come, come, do not delay! We must send word to the villa at once that they may come running to meet you even as his father met the prodigal son."

Her tongue ran so fast that the children had no chance to ask questions. A crowd now gathered about them, and when Teresina had explained the cause of the excitement and joy, sympathetic bystanders rushed to send word to the villa, seven miles away, and to spread the good news that the children of the Marchese Grifoni, for whom the police had been searching every town in Italy for two months, had now appeared in Padua.

"It is not for nothing that Saint Anthony is the patron saint of all who suffer loss," said the pious ones, and many a candle was gratefully offered on his shrine that day.

When her joy had a little subsided, Teresina gazed with horror at the Twins. They were indeed a terrifying spectacle. Ragged, thin, encrusted with dirt, with their toes sticking through their worn-out shoes, it is no wonder that she did not at once recognise the children of the Marchese. Grasping them by the hands as if she would never again let them go, Teresina hurried them toward the Hotel Due Croci Bianche, which opened upon the square, followed by crowds of interested spectators. The landlord himself, when the news reached him, came out to greet the wanderers and conduct them to a room.

Teresina went with them, giving orders right and left as she flew down the long corridor.

"It is for the Marchese Grifoni!" she cried to the bewildered servants, as she hustled the children before her to the bath. "Bring soap, bring towels, bring food, and for the love of Saint Anthony keep the wires hot to the villa. Never mind the cost, for the lost is found. They will reward you well. Tell them, for the love of Heaven, to bring clothes for the Signorina and Don Beppo, and hurry, hurry, hurry!"

Then she shut the door upon her charges, and the process of purification began. She rang the bell furiously a few moments later, and, opening the door a crack, handed the servant who answered it a bundle, hastily wrapped in newspaper.

"Their clothes," she said briefly. "The Marchesa must not see them. Burn them at once!"

For one hour or more she scrubbed and shampooed, and all but boiled the wanderers alive in her frantic efforts to get them clean before their mother should be able to reach them.

At last a carriage, drawn by a pair of steaming black horses, dashed up to the hotel, and the beautiful Marchesa, pale but radiant, sprang out and, attended by the landlord himself, hurried to the room where her lost ones waited to embrace her! Teresina opened the door, and, stepping into the hall, left the mother and children together with no human eye to see that meeting! Red-eyed herself, and wiping her nose vigorously on her apron, she went down to tell the footman all the news, and to get the bundle of clothes for the children, which in the haste and excitement had been left in the carriage.

An hour later, the Marchesa and two very clean and happy children came out of the hotel, followed by Teresina. The coachman, grinning, as Teresina said, "like a cracked melon," greeted the children as if he were an old friend, and the Marchesa, standing in her carriage, scattered tips with a lavish hand. They drove away with the landlord bowing from the doorway, and the crowd shouting vivas as long as the carriage was in sight.

It was a long drive over beautiful, winding roadways to the villa, and every inch of the way the Marchesa sat with her arms clasped about her darlings telling them of their father, who was still in Florence conducting the search, of the baby, who had six teeth and was fat as butter, and hearing from them the tale of their adventures, while Teresina beamed at them from the opposite seat.

At last they rounded a well-remembered curve in the road, and there, shining down on them from the summit of a hill overlooking the village, was their own white, vine-covered villa. The children shouted with joy when they saw it, and Beppina threw a kiss.

Then they heard a great shouting down the road. All the village had come out to greet the children of their beloved Marchesa. Old and young, they swarmed about the carriage, shouting "Ben trovati," which means "Welcome," and tossing flowers at the feet of the returned travellers. Ah, what a happy time it was!

At last the carriage stood before the loggia of the villa, and when his old dog, barking with joy, came bounding out to meet them, Beppo, who had been dry-eyed and brave through all the dreadful weeks, buried his head in Tonio's shaggy fur and gave way to tears.

After the baby had been kissed, and the servants greeted, and all the dear, familiar places visited once more, it was time for supper, and, oh, what a supper it was! The cook, the moment the wonderful news had reached the villa, had flown to the kitchen, and there she had cooked all their favourite dishes. There were artichokes for Beppina, and stufato for Beppo, and a cake as soft and light as thistle-down for dessert. In the evening they received a telegram of welcome from their dear Babbo in Florence, for the good news had been flashed across the wires to him and all the servants in the Grifoni palace were rejoicing too.

When bedtime came, instead of lying down upon straw, or a husk mattress, the Twins had their own mother to tuck them in their own white beds in their own dear, clean rooms, and then to sing them to sleep as she had done when they were little, little children.

Long after they were safe in dreamland, the Marchesa lingered beside their beds, and then, throwing herself upon her knees before the image of the Madonna in her own room, she poured out her grateful heart in thanksgiving to that other Mother who had lived and suffered too.

Lucy Fitch Perkins – A Short Biography

One of American literature's almost forgotten names, but in the early 20th Century a wildly popular authoress is Lucy Fitch Perkins, author and illustrator of children's books and originator of the popular Twins series. She was born on 12th July 1865 in Maples, Indiana. Her father, Appleton Howe Fitch, had graduated from Amherst college and spent his professional career working as a teacher and eventually become principle of a school in Chicago. Shortly before his daughter's birth he exchanged teaching for the lumber business and the family relocated to Maples for its forestry. Her mother was Elizabeth Bennett. Both her parents were Puritan, and ensured that a key value in their children's upbringing was education. Though Lucy and her sisters were home-schooled, their parents made sure that they frequently visited Massachusetts and their ancestral home, approximately twenty-five miles out of Boston, where the girls spent time in school so they might experience social interaction with others their age.

Eventually, in 1879, the family permanently removed to the property in Massachusetts, and the girls spent the remainder of their school years here. Lucy displayed early talent in writing and drawing and when she graduated from high school she chose to attend the art school at the Boston Museum of Fine Arts, where she was a student for three years. After graduating, she found employment illustrating for the Prang Educational Company of Boston, where she stayed for a year before moving on to a teaching post at the Pratt Institute, then only recently established.

During these years she made the first inroads into a career in this field, illustrating a translation of The Goose Girl, a German fairy tale made known as Tale no. 89 in the Brothers Grimm's collections, and A Book of Joys: The Story of a New England Summer, which she both wrote and illustrated.

Lucy spent four years working at the Pratt Institute, continuing her own studies while carrying out her teaching duties. She writes of her time there as "happy", enjoying the combination of working on her own talents, while passing them on to others. Then, in 1881, she married a young architect named Dwight Heald Perkins. They had met years earlier while they were both studying in Boston. Their married home was to be in Evanston, Chicago, where Lucy gave birth to Eleanor Ellis and Lawrence Bradford Perkins. They lived here for several years, Lucy working as an illustrator for various publishers and magazines and Dwight as a teacher at the Massachusetts Institute of Technology. They were both active members of their community, and Lucy writes that they "lived fully in the events and thought currents of the time".

She was forty-eight when she was approached by a publisher friend who, aware and impressed by her talents as both an illustrator, which was her profession, and as a writer, which he knew through correspondence, urged her to write. He was so earnest that she thought of an idea for a children's book the next morning, and she immediately set to work making sketches and preparing the idea for presentation. The publisher came to dinner at their house the next evening and she took the opportunity to show him. He responded "go ahead and write it, and I want it". That book was The Dutch Twins, the first in what became a popular series. Using simple language, vivid imagery, stories of adventure and simple moral issues, the stories gently introduced their readers to other countries and cultures, and some of their basic differences with America. Though she had previously published The Goose Girl and A Book of Joys, there is a shift in emphasis from the illustrations to the writing; previously, the illustrations were the primary focus of the books, whereas now, they merely complimented the vividness of her imagery in writing.

Lucy later wrote of the Twins series that they were borne of two key ideas. The first, of "the necessity for mutual respect and understanding between people of different nationalities" if there was ever to be global peace, she felt particularly resonated in her own country, where "all the nations of the earth are represented in the population" (indeed, the term 'melting pot' which we use to describe civilisations where several different cultures are to be found living together was just being coined as a descriptive term in America). The second of these two ideas was that it was possible to hold a child's attention, even when writing about big, complex ideas, so long as the language and story were engaging. As an example, in The Dutch Twins, Lucy touches upon proto-feminist ideas through a childish discussion between her twins about the ships sailing past them as the fish with their grandfather on the dyke near their home.

"I think I'll be a sea captain when I'm big," said Kit.
"So will I,", said Kat.
"Girls can't," said Kit.
But Grandfather shook his head and said: "You can't tell what a girl may be by the time she's four feet and a half high and is called Katrina. There's no telling what girls will do anyway."

This particular interest in Katrina's potential is reflected in Lucy's involvement in several social and artistic reform groups in Chicago, including the Chicago Women's Club and the League of Women Voters.

She saw the need for the themes of each story to be made vivid by their effect on the individuals involved. For Kit and Kat, young siblings growing up together and playing together, witnessing the ships sailing in front of them, the realisation of the female potential is made more vivid than if it were merely being explained to them in a classroom. By witnessing the ships sailing for America, England and elsewhere, Kat sees how the profession of sea-captain is a means for adventure and exploration, and so the injustice of the default, immediate "girls can't" is made painfully apparent. Similarly, to the American children reading the tale, since they can relate to the children's play and childishness, the messages is made more accessible. Lucy writes "I visited a school in Chicago where children of twenty-seven different nationalities were herded in one building, and marveled at what the teachers were able to accomplish. It seemed to me it might help in the fusing process if these children could be interested in the best qualities which they bring to our shores." Over two decades, Lucy wrote 26 stories in the Twins series. The popular children's author Beverly Cleary notes that the Twins series engaged her as an early reader, and ultimately served as inspiration for her writing. Alongside the Twins series, Lucy illustrated Edith Ogden Harrison's fairy tales, which were published in the 1900s.

As she well understood, it remains important to teach children early of the value of other cultures, and the history of one's own. Her writing can still be used as effective learning tools for their playful language, humour clarity still engages a young audience. Moreover, the sketches afford a visual representation of clothing and thereby a subtle hint at costume design for those children so enamoured with the stories that they wish to act them out. The Irish Twins, in particular, addresses "the abuses of absentee landlordism" which partly caused the mass immigration from Ireland to America at the country's birth.

Lucy died while holidaying in Pasadena, California, on 18th March 1937. She was seventy-two. Her books have been translated into several international languages, for their cultural importance is borderless. She writes that she "tried to contribute something to the making of Americans by an appreciation of what has been done in the past to make America what it is today, and of the constructive qualities in the material at hand with which we must build the nation of the future." This altruism and desire for social and cultural awareness and reform survives her, and though America went though almost a century of widespread social oppression, racism and xenophobia, as new writers and activists seek reform, we would do well to reflect on the pertinence and relevance of Perkins's work.

www.ingramcontent.com/pod-product-compliance
Lightning Source LLC
Chambersburg PA
CBHW061505170626
46811CB00004B/1617

* 9 7 8 1 7 8 3 9 4 6 0 3 7 *